# THE RODEO OF DOOM

# THE RODEO OF DOOM

by
## MIGUEL LASALA

Copyright © 2013 by Miguel Lasala
Cover design and layout by 2013 Miguel Lasala
Editor: Margaret A. Harrell
Additional Copy Editing: Michele Taylor Ponson

Whiskey Bay Press
Carencro, Louisiana.
whiskeybaypress@gmail.com

ISBN-10: 0615802109
ISBN-13: 978-0615802107

*To the late Tommy Ray Ayres,*
*who told me to sit down in a chair*
*and get it done*

## EDITOR'S NOTE

*On June 26, 2384, Henry Fields disappeared into the mountains of Neo Mexico. The following manuscript was produced entirely from his last known voice recordings.*

*Margaret A. Harrell*

## A WARNING TO THE READER

*Do not attempt to read this in a public setting. Any weirdness that may come your way will not be the fault of yours truly.*

*Henry Fields*

# 1

Today is the last day of the semester. It also marks the end of my tenth year as what is referred to as an adjunct, an appendage, a necessary but unidentifiable tentacle in the College of Architecture at Andreas Tangen University in Los Angeles.

I'll skip the bullshit and just say it: universities are dead. What you see playing out here is a charade. Anyone with any sense at all can get to the truth without all the hierarchy of the institution. Access to knowledge is actually slowed down in the universities, and anything accidentally stumbled upon through research is suppressed until further notice.

Office hours.

I tell my students at the beginning of each semester, "If you need me, I'll be at Louie's Tavern." My hours are written in blue ballpoint pen on a receipt and taped to my office door. Underneath it, there's a map with a big X marking Louie's Tavern, my true office. Sometimes they come down and complain, but at least there's music and drinks that offer a little distraction.

The truth.

You can smell it everywhere like the rotting flesh of a dead dog; although, I've found that almost no one dares to acknowledge it. That's the way it is these days, the world so obliviously turned on its ass. But they'll tell you nothing has changed even though the war just ended, and many more threaten to flare up any day now. For hundreds of years, they said it was coming—the big III was supposed to wipe us all out. Well, they fucked that one up, too, so what else is new? World War III was supposed to be the big final "fuck you" to God from the human race. Boy, did that whole thing go to shit. It just turned into one goddamned fight to the death with nothing less than a bunch of robots, or whatever they call those flying machines from hell that all seem to malfunction more than anything else.

When it looked liked combat was going to become face to face, not many humans could be found to fill the uniforms. It had been so long since any U.S. citizen had been killed in combat that the idea seemed silly to most people. The bigwigs threw all kinds of threats around, but in the end, not many people were all that keen on fighting. The same old tactics no longer worked following the golden period of so-called enlightenment. It's not that people became holy or anything like that; they just didn't want to die prematurely anymore. Besides, with the substances around today, you can live to be 200 if you want to—not that hard—so people figured, "Fuck war, we have to make money if we're going to be running around the earth this long."

Times have changed, my friend. I know because I read history, but most people don't get it. They still complain. They say, "When will there ever be enough time?" I like to fuck with these people in particular. I tell them, "Two centuries ago you'd be dust in a grave right now at 118, so why not try something other than complaining for a change?"

Myself, I think I'm somewhere around 137. I forget, but I don't forget the recipe unearthed by an old med school friend of mine, Bill Macy. He found it in an ancient Chinese text. The big secret to a long and fruitful life was there all along for those who wanted to find it, but then of course, the text disappeared along with any and all traces of Bill. Now, only a handful of people, including myself, know the recipe. Only other problem is two out of the five ingredients no longer exist.

At home, I have a special safe built into the wall, but it's not for cash or jewels or guns. What I have is enough EP14 brewing in there to keep me going way past these strip mall flunkies that buy up all the watered-down TA65 tinctures on sale at Safeway.

If you asked me, aside from the paunch, I look forty-five on a good day. Some days, I even think I look like a middle-aged Tom Selleck, mustache and all. But no one around here has any idea who that is. They don't scan the history files. They just sit around complaining like angry children even though they are, in actuality, old bastards. Fuck them. They don't deserve any of my EP14. Not one of them. I've only shared it with a couple of co-eds, but that's another story I'll get into later.

This afternoon was my last stuck here till the summer break, and I had last-minute meetings with nervous and manic second-year students. Earlier in the day, I had my own problems getting in to see the director. It's a question of too little pay. I tell him, "This is my goddamned twentieth career so far. I'm ready to retire. Enough of this adjunct bullshit; let's talk tenure and promotion."

But the director waves me off like a pimp: "All in due time, Henry."

Not to mention when I awoke today, I had a bad case of the runs. The EP14 can have a way with the stomach. Many Alka-Seltzers later and halfway through a cigar, I drove the twenty seconds it takes to get to school with the windows down. While I drive sirens are blasting and screeching through the canopies of the trees like giant invisible birds that are coming to eat all of our heads off for keeping the lie alive, and getting paid for it at that. The lie being, higher education is somehow useful.

It was a false alarm.

A bunch of renegade physics students got their hands on a Tornado Machine and damn near took the roof off the math building. Good thing for the kill switch.

These days, I wear loud shirts just like Tom Selleck did four hundred years ago. I let them do the talking for me. I'm an architect now, but I like to think I could have been a private eye. It's always been my dream—helicopters, guns, intrigue, and women in bikinis hanging off of my arms while I save the world. Why not? What's your dream?

But I took a wrong turn somewhere. I got mixed up with architecture for some reason, and the profession seems to have taken a wrong turn like the practice of medicine over the years. It's become corrupt and nonsensical. Now, we can see the obvious problems right under our noses if we're paying any kind of attention, but no one wants to talk about them.

So, if it's true that the banks are purposefully trying to crush themselves in order to establish a one-world currency, then the major and minor professions are following suit. It would seem that they're all doing their damnedest to guarantee that they become obsolete, and again, like in medicine, only madmen seem to be attracted to architecture these days. That's what I can tell from my view anyway.

It all started in 2001 with Building 7. Some thought it was an inside job. Not the case. We still live in a time when buildings literally vanish from sight in broad daylight, and nobody seems to have a problem with it. Now the talk is that the little men in the sky, a.k.a the Clouds, are responsible. Evidence points to a training video game that their youth have been playing. Only difference from our games is that their targets are real. Who knows, the wiry little turds up in the sky have been a nuisance ever since they made their big coming-out party on Xmas Eve of 2345, so it's no real surprise.

Today, not only do buildings vanish, but people go missing all the time. If you listen closely, you can hear the dead and dying and nameless scratch away at your screen door at night. Yeah, another thing I forgot to mention, ghosts are everywhere now for some of us. They say that being able to see them may be a side effect of the EP14. But who knows? That's just how it is these days. But some still say they don't build buildings like they used to—they don't handle fire like they used to, the steel they use now isn't the same; it's from China, and it melts and degenerates with ease. So it's all going up in flames—buildings, infrastructure, laws, rights, good-looking coeds. They all seem to be vanishing or going crazy in the year of our Lord 2384.

# 2

When I walk back to school from Louie's Tavern after lunch, I walk quickly against the dusty wind, my hair standing straight up, and as I reach for my cigar, I hear a thump followed by a crash, like several 18-wheelers falling from the sky. It was the math building, finally pulverized. No one knows exactly what happened. Shoddy construction, or was it the Clouds, or the Tesla Gang on campus playing with their magnetic wave machine they built last summer with grant money from The Science Incentive Group?

But what really bothers me is that I'm the only person I know that has been an adjunct professor for over ten years. This, no doubt, has to do with the fact that I'm a graduate of the same university that I am now employed. Obviously, this makes me a *nincompoop that can't be trusted*. In my undergraduate days, I was a letter writer. Most of these letters were written between the hours of three and five in the morning and addressed to the university president. Red flags surfaced, and I imagine have been working against me ever since.

The Ball Dropper.

After lunch, I had a meeting with a ball dropper. Why didn't I tell him he was a ball dropper, and why did I insult him while grading his project? He said he overheard me say that he was a talentless nut while I discussed his project with my colleague Frank Betterton.

I told him to think it over when I met with him at his studio desk. I told him I meant that he did, in fact, have talent but wasn't using any of it, hence, ball dropping. So then I'm told that the teaching wasn't there, I was always wasting everyone's time in class, and he didn't think I had any idea what I was talking about half the time, which unfortunately, is always a possibility.

Teaching.

I'll tell you about teaching. It's about being on the spot all day long in front of crowds of hung-over students either watching your every move or nodding off while others look like they are planning attacks on your property, person, and/or sanity.

After my ball-dropping meeting, I walk to Betterton's office and take a seat. He's on the phone with his feet up on the desk. I pick up an ancient Peter Greenaway book and flip through it while he slams the phone into the cradle; his white mustache is awake and moving. His green eyes are wrapped in pink goo.

"My daughter is an imbecile," he tells me. "I waited to have children till as late as biologically possible, and now

I'm faced with the terrifying prospect of being driven half crazy by my 16-year-old child. She doesn't rest. She's energetic and full of lopsided logic. I don't know if I can live long enough to bring this kid around. My 10-year-old boy is applying to an international business school in Japan3, and Cindy seems hell-bent on following my path and will be locked up in Angola State Pen by the time she's 18."

Betterton leans back and runs his hand through his cloud of solid white hair, takes a deep breath, exhaling through his nose as his mustache flattens out, then springs back.

"Cigarette?" I ask him.

"I quit thirty-five years ago, but that sounds like a great idea right now."

Betterton leans forward, picking a cigarette out of the pack, his chair groaning under his weight.

"I want you to recognize your position here, Henry. Despite your age, you're still new at this, and you need to make sure you try and milk it while you can."

"How do you mean?"

"Listen, when I was adjunct here, I'd be smoking with students out on the hill while meetings were going on. Tanner would come looking for me, gasping for air and pink in the cheeks, and I'd be deep in conversation with nineteen-year-old co-eds while handing out Marlboros. Grades would be due, and at the last minute I would throw darts at the drawings on the wall. The ones I hit were my only A's. You only get excused once when you start out; then it's only after tenure when you can completely disregard responsibility again."

# 3

Just after speaking with Betterton, I walk out into parking lot #oo25 and find a girl lying unconscious outside the english building. Another girl was by her side and yelling at her, "Can you hear me? Say something!"

After I walked up, others began to arrive on foot. We waited. An ambulance was on its way. I knew the girl. Her name was Natalie, and I had given her some of the EP14 a few weeks before. She had spent the night, a few times. Now she was turning green. I knelt down and spoke to her.

"Natalie. You there?" She wasn't a bad-looking girl for thirty-five. I assured everyone all around that I was a doctor, in a previous life sure, almost fifty years before, but what the hell? Once a doctor, always a doctor.

I stood up. "Now, listen here, I'm a doctor and I have an idea of what might be the problem, but I'll need everyone to step back and give me some space to work."

I knelt down on the hard ground again and reached for the vial in my corduroy coat pocket. I took the EP14, opened it, then poured a few drops under her tongue.

Someone spoke up. "Hey, what is he doing? He's not a doctor; he's an adjunct in the Architecture Department."

After putting the vial away, I watched her face. Nothing.

Then someone standing there said, "I'm sorry, but you need to leave this to the emergency personnel, mister."

I knew it would come soon, the jolt of life, so I stayed put with my eyes steady on her. They would all thank me in the end. They'd write something up in the paper the next day: 137-YEAR-OLD ADJUNCT SAVES CO-ED FROM CERTAIN DEATH.

I turned around and looked up at them. "Will you people please shut the hell up? As you will see in a few minutes, I have this situation under control."

Then someone else said, "He's just an adjunct. We should get him away from her."

That's when they grabbed me and stood me up and I found my director standing in the crowd, facing me.

"Henry, what in the hell are you doing? I could have you fired for this."

"I was just trying to help the girl before it's too late," I said.

"Well, look at her. She's dead, Henry. Looks like she's been dead for half an hour, at least. Look at her. She's already turned green."

Then someone said, "He put something in her mouth." And another said, "Yeah, he opened her mouth and put something in it."

The director's forehead was wet with sweat. His mouth trembled before he spoke. "Is this true?"

"Check his pockets," someone else said.

"Hand it over, Henry."

Down the street we heard the sirens screaming through the trees again and everyone looked in their direction.

I ran for it. My ancient Camaro SS 396 was illegally parked not far off.

"Get him," someone yelled.

I had about eight paces in front of the crowd when I managed to get into the Red Beast. They crowded onto the hood, screaming at me.

"Fuck you, you silly bastards," I said. "I'll kill all of you. I swear I'll take you all down."

I took the EP14, swallowed a few drops, then cranked up the awful beast. Anyone crazy enough to have been standing behind me quickly shot out of the way like spooked deer as the first crack of the engine punched their eardrums. Even two hundred years ago, only the most depraved, inhuman maniacs could be found driving ancient chariots like this. Luckily for me, my great-great-grandfather was one of the few mad scientists hell-bent on knowing what it was like to truly experience the gerund we like to call "driving". Even the sleek magnet coasters from his day all but ruined the experience, and he and a group of hell raisers scavenged for years in order to bring back to life the truest expression of human freedom, to blast down the freeway in a roaring wild hell beast on wheels at ten miles to the gallon of the most expensive fuel on earth; and God bless his crazy soul for keeping it in the family.

When I backed up, I did so sharply only to slam on the brakes, which sent all the geeks on the hood falling off in all directions. After that, only one turkey was still clinging on with his fingers like a rodeo clown when I beamed my eyes into his.

"You goddamn degenerate!" I yelled at him. "I'll find you, and you're going to pay for the goddamned bodywork. You hear me?"

As he slid off of the hood I saw that his ass had made a bowl in the middle of my candy-apple-red baby.

Then there was a knock at the driver's side window. It was my director.

"You're finished, Henry. You hear me? You're finished here."

I smiled at him, then cut the wheel and floored the bastard, which sent white smoke up into the air and pure horror into the hearts of anyone within a hundred yards. Considering everything, it felt like the right thing to do.

# 4

The next morning, I got a call from the newspaper. The girl lived and the doctors were confused. They couldn't explain it. She had a heart attack and tissue had ruptured, but somehow, she didn't seem to suffer any ill effects from it. They still had her under observation in the ICU, and they wanted to speak with me about whatever it was that I had done. Before I went down there to meet the reporter, I locked every bit of the EP14 into my safe.

The summer of 2384 was promising to be spectacular. Tanner, my director, called before I left my place, and he apologized and promised a promotion when I returned in the fall. I was someone they didn't want to lose. He assured me that I would be made a handsome offer, but for now, just take it easy, enjoy the summer, and report back on August 13.

I gave nothing up to the reporter kid that I met at the hospital. He was nervous and probably only about twenty-five from what I could tell.

"There was talk of a substance you might have given her. Can you elaborate on that?"

I smiled a dimple-faced Tom Selleck grin for him. "Just a little holy water I keep with me for special occasions."

"But bystanders claimed the substance looked green."

"What are you telling me, son? Haven't you ever seen green holy water?"

He looked horrified.

"Which church do you attend in these uncertain days?"

He had no answer.

"Clear as glass holy water—put that down. I gave the girl holy water. A little of the Lord can go a long way, you know? Don't you believe in miracles? You see, I've been touched by a higher power. That is all."

I stood up and left the kid chewing his pencil. I walked to Louie's Tavern. The Red Beast was still in the shop being attended to.

# 5

I took a stool and ordered two hamburgers and two Old
Düsseldorfs. The news was on and the girl's father was
talking about the incident. He wanted to thank me. The
bartender looked up.

"What the hell is that all about, Henry?"

"Nothing."

"You saved somebody's life?"

"I guess you could say that. Sure, I saved her."

Just then, I remembered her naked thighs wrapped
around my neck. It made me quiver. I'd have to let the
steam die down; then I'd have to pay her a little visit.

Then Betterton walked in and took a stool next to me.
He looked nervous and his forehead was pink and wet with
sweat like he had just run over in a trot.

"You know anything about the Mark 5?"

"Sure, they're a bunch of crooked pharmaceutical salesmen."

"Well, some of their boys came around looking for you today. They didn't know you were an adjunct and that you didn't have to attend our end-of-the-semester meeting. They just stood in front of the conference room for an hour, thinking you were inside. There were three of them, big as running backs, with one little squirmy-looking Chinaman in a green suit."

"What would those kooks want with me?"

"It's the liquid that brought the girl back, Henry. They're into that kind of shit, and they're going to try and get it from you."

Betterton ordered a beer. "...Anyway, you need to get out of here. I'm pretty sure they're hanging outside of your office right now, and soon they'll see your map."

"Fuck them," I said. "I have nothing but holy water for them. If they're already believers, then they won't need my help anyway."

Then, just like that, they were standing inside Louie's Tavern, and the little man in the green suit walked up to me without a word and touched me on the neck with something that knocked me out deader to the world than Novocain 4000.

# 6

I woke up in a familiar room. It looked like mine. It was mine. It was my living room. Betterton was there, too, and he was still sleeping on the ground. The little man in the green suit sat before us in my easy chair. His goons stood behind him.

"We're here to make you an offer, Mr. Fields."

I fished out my cigar and took my time lighting it as I sat up. "Is that right? What's the offer?"

"Despite what many believe, we are not criminals, Mr. Fields. We are businessmen."

"These days, what's the difference?"

"We promise to make you an offer you can't refuse for your supply of EP14. We know you have it, and unlike you, we know its potential."

"Listen, it was just holy water."

"If it's just holy water, then the price stands. We'll give you $235,000 for whatever supply you have left."

"And what if I don't have anymore?"

"Oh, you do, Mr. Henry Fields. We looked at your records. You're going to be 147 this month, and no one has managed to live that long since Helmet Schnook, who died at the ripe old age of 198, and we know his long life had everything to do with a certain green substance."

"Well, what if I don't need the money, friend? Besides I just got promoted. How do you like that?"

"Maybe that is all true, but we have some information that might affect your chances with the tenure committee. We know that you were sexually involved with, not one, but three students in the last ten years."

"Blackmail. I often wondered how it worked," I said.

"Call it what you like, Mr. Fields."

"What if I said that I loved them all? I loved them with all of my heart."

"Say what you like, but you can quickly see that a man of your age will have a difficult time trying to start yet another career if this kind of information were to start floating around."

Finally, Betterton came to and yelled out, "What the fuck happened?" He looked at the little man in the chair.

"Holy Jesus, you little twerp." He stood up and ran for him, but the goons grabbed him and slapped him around a bit, then threw him onto the couch.

"No worries here, Betterton," I said, "Save your strength. These gentlemen were just leaving."

The Chinaman was smiling like he had just fucked a pig on a Friday night and got away with it. He put a card on the coffee table; then they all filed out one by one, until the little man reached the door, bowed, then disappeared.

# 7

That night, I reviewed my bank account statements. I was down in all areas and it would cost a grand to fix the Red Beast. On the coffee table, I had a letter explaining that my student loans from medical school were out of deferment, and a payment of $1250 was due at the end of the month. I managed to keep the loans in deferment for the last fifty-two years, but now the bastards were coming for me. I thought I'd die before they could get to me, but thanks to the EP14, I would have to pay up or go to jail because that's what they do with scratchers these days. They come for you in the middle of the night and demand payment. A few hundred years ago, they'd just called you until your head fell off, but now they grab you out of bed and send you off to a camp somewhere where you're forced to teach everything you know in exchange for credit toward your debt. At ten dollars an hour, it would take a thousand years to make a dent. So much for the American Dream.

I looked up at the safe hidden in the wall. "How long do you want to live anyway, I asked myself?" Why not sell it all and run off to some remote island and become another Magnum, P.I.? With the money, I could pay off my debt and still have enough to live out my last few years in comfort. If I quit the EP14 system right now, I'd probably only last a few years anyway. Might as well do them in style.

I looked through my wallet and found the Chinaman's card. Joseph Ping was his name. On the phone, I set up a meeting, but it wouldn't be for two days. I needed time to think and make plans. After all, what I was selling was going to be my own life.

# 8

In the morning the Red Beast was ready. I took it for a drive out into the country, way past civilization, and went to where the ducks gathered in a remote clearing. I figured I was too far out for a signal, but a call managed to come through on the dash. It was Natalie's father. His daughter had taken a turn for the worst. There were complications. He wanted me to come and see her and do whatever I had done before. He didn't think she would make it otherwise.

Natalie was unconscious when I arrived. I brought flowers and handed them to her father. Small magnets were placed all over her body. They ran up in straight lines following the meridian points.

Her father was sitting down in a yellow chair with a cane resting on his knee. He was only about a hundred but had been using cheap system stuff and he wasn't going to last long. There were tubes running directly into Natalie's veins. She was set up with Demerol and Amyl Nitrite. Garbage. The human body is made up of cells, and when the cells are hungry, if you don't feed them, they'll start eating up the body's energy supply. The simple trick is to overdose the supply often, but only EP14 can do the job.

I had counted 108 vials left in my safe. If used with efficiency, a vial could last a year at a single drop a day, 365 drops per vial. I explained everything to her father. "This is all I can spare."

I handed him ten vials and would keep ten for myself. Back home, I had packed up the remaining eighty-eight for the kooks in exchange for $235,000 in cash. Why not skim off the top? The bastards.

When the doctor left the room, we gave it to her. Soon she would be home, and I'd be in another country doing somersaults off a high dive with a Speedo on. We were all going to be all right. I was certain of it.

## 9

Then I saw them, the ghosts. They walked into my house and sat down on the furniture that night. They wanted to talk.

"Don't sell the EP14," they said. "You will regret it. Many need it, and if you give it to the Mark 5, they are going to use it in evil ways."

Like with all ghosts, communication is hazy. The reception doesn't always come in clear, and sometimes they don't make any sense at all. I could only pick up a few things from time to time, but often, I would just ignore them by turning up the volume on the stereo. I was drinking beer and listening to *Chicago Live in 75*, and I didn't feel like a conference with the dead anyway. I was in planning mode.

When they didn't get the message that I didn't want them there, I told them, "You're all just a bunch of sorry losers. Why don't you find an old house somewhere to haunt? Why are you waltzing in here uninvited anyway?"

"But you did invite us by taking the EP14," the leader of the group said. "We are subjects from Mark 5; they are creating a purgatorial prison for the dead and preventing us from leaving this world. They're holding us in an illegal compound and suck energy from our spirits in order to negotiate with the Clouds; that's why we are so weak."

"Sounds a lot like life," I said.

"Yes, but we must take them down, and we need someone on the other side to help us."

I dosed heavily that night in order to communicate with them, but found myself getting weirder and weirder by the minute, until I fell on my couch and lost consciousness.

# 10

Later that morning I awoke to news about Natalie on the oxygen screen. Her recovery was a huge hit around the world and her father was able to take her home the night before. Soon they would have her on all the daytime talk shows. Good for her, I thought.

I put on my lucky Hawaiian shirt and decided not to shave. A five o'clock shadow gave the proper message. I wanted these people to know I meant business and wouldn't allow any bullshit. I watched half an episode of *Magnum, P.I.*, then took the Red Beast to the Black Garter on Ocean Parkway.

I had the stuff locked up in the trunk, and I ordered a Bloody Mary with gin and Schizandra juice. Inside my coat, I was wearing my ancient Colt .45 M1911 with one in the chamber.

There was only one other character sitting at the bar when I arrived at ten o'clock in the morning. Stanley, like always, sat drinking scotch in a black velvet jogging suit. Each finger on both hands held a gold ring. On his right ring finger, he had a Super Bowl ring flashing in the dark room. He wore blue Aviators and didn't say much, just nodded when I sat down. The bartender wore a red tuxedo jacket. He stood there washing glasses when the goons entered the bar.

"Mr. Fields, you're doing the right thing."

"Yeah, I don't care about that. Just show me the money."

One of the goons had a briefcase. He opened it. The pink bills shone like salmon filets in the chrome-plated case.

We walked out into the blue sky. I popped the trunk and we made the switch. Everything went smoothly. They had a black car waiting and they all got in and drove off. I put the case in the trunk and locked it. I had expected a shootout, but then I decided that I had watched too many episodes of *Magnum, P.I.* The world didn't operate like that anymore. Some things were simple; some things operated without high drama or violence. I felt good and returned to my stool to finish my drink.

Now Stanley spoke up: "What did you just do? Sell your soul?"

"No, Pop, just some holy water."

"Those were Mark 5 men. They're the gatekeepers. I know because I've been to the other side. I was locked up in limbo for years until I found a way out."

"Well, Pop, I'd love to hear all about it, but I have a plane to catch. My new life starts now."

"Now, son, you can't take a payoff from those people. You'll be doomed. You have to burn whatever it is they gave you. It's contaminated, you hear me. It's blood money, and they'll own you if you do."

I looked at Stanley. His eyes were glaring at me.

"What the hell are you taking about?" I said as I stood up to leave.

"Okay, don't listen, but don't say I didn't warn you."

He was still talking when I made my way out to the parking lot and found my Red Beast gone from the lot. I still had my keys but not much else. Inside my coat, only the empty holster rested against my ribs. The swine had taken the Red Beast and my .45 without me having any idea.

# 11

I tracked down Betterton at his lake house in Genevieve. He was sitting in the hot tub when he picked up the phone.

"They got everything."

"Sounds like your summer is getting off to a good start."

"I need wheels. Can I borrow your roadster?"

"No way in hell. Cindy's off to boot camp this summer; you can use her car."

"What is it?"

"It's a brown Geo Prizm with orange and yellow racing stripes."

"Jesus."

I took a taxi service out to his lake house and found him in a bathrobe with a towel on his head when I walked in. I sat down and told him everything.

That's a beautiful mess you got yourself into, Henry. What's the plan from here? Go after the Mark 5?"

"No one fucks with my Camaro."

"Look, try not to destroy the Geo in the process; it's not much, but it's a car."

I took the opportunity to ask for a small loan.

"I'm flat till August. I got all the pay up front on the nine months. I'm just floating till next school year. Go see the girl and her father. You saved her life; the least they can do is give you a loan."

He was right. I had no other choice but to try them for a favor.

# 12

The Geo maxed out at fifty miles an hour. I banged on the steering wheel. "Goddamn you, you little bastard. If you make one dint on the Red Beast, I'll hang you from a telephone pole by your balls."

All the exterior lights were on when I reached Natalie's father's place even though it was only 4 p.m. I snuck around the back to Natalie's window to speak with her first and see what she thought about my situation. There was no answer. Front door was the same. Dead silent—only cicadas could be heard chanting in the trees up above.

I tried the door and found it unlocked. No ventilation systems were active, and the smell of rotting food hit me as I entered.

A meal was set up on the table. The wine had been opened with glasses all around for a celebration, but something stopped this dinner party prematurely. No one touched the food. They had all been gathered up and taken away, but Natalie was a smart girl. I knew where she hid her drugs. There would be her stash of EP14 there if I knew my girl as well as I thought.

I hit my shin on the coffee table when I crossed the living room. Bright pain was followed by a few drops of blood running down my leg.

Inside her bedroom, I looked around. There were all the things left over from her childhood: Teddy bears, a laser gun, robots—all ancient and sitting in dust on a book case amongst old, left-over circuit boards.

In one of the light machines, I found a bag of L-148 pills, but not much else besides a little brown powder left over from her high school days. If they had gotten to her, then maybe she just gave them the stuff, but that didn't get me any closer to figuring out where she was now.

Then I got an idea. Tanner was the only person who could possibly help me out. He didn't need to know much, just enough to get him to part with some cash. I grabbed the low-voltage laser gun and took it with me. It wasn't much, but it could make a man shit his pants at twenty yards if he meant ill intent. The government had handed them out over the years to help curb the rape epidemic that had spread across the country following the illegalization of porn.

# 13

I took the little car down the road that led to the city dump. At an iron wheel mailbox, I took a left and bounced in and out of potholes and mud on the old road till I reached Tanners' egg-shaped house. I parked and walked past the rabbit cages and the chicken coops. Tanner was in shorts and stringing up a fishing pole on the porch when I found him.

"Henry, what the hell brings you here? I'm just getting ready for some fishing down at the pond. I've got plenty of beer here. You should join me. Wait, I'll get you a pole."

He ran off and I sat down. It was late in the day and the sun was only an inch or two from the horizon. When we walked over to the bank of the pond, he took off his sandals.

"You know anything about the pineal gland, Henry?"

"Sure, it's a little pinecone in our heads, right in the center."

"Do you know what it can do if activated?

"No idea, Tanner."

"It's the key to longevity, my friend. The ancients knew about it, but they've been hiding its secrets from us for hundreds, if not thousands, of years."

I cracked open a beer.

"Now, watch what I do." He stretched his arms out and stared right at the sun for about three minutes; then he looked at me with a dreamy look on his face.

"Try it, Henry. It'll do you some good."

"Won't it burn my fucking eyeballs out of my head?"

"No, boy, not at this time of day. That's why I come out here at sunset."

I put my beer down and removed my shoes. I was there for a loan, and if it meant playing along with some New Age bullshit, then it was a small price to pay.

"Now, because you're new at this, I recommend only thirty seconds for you. Anymore and you'll get a headache."

My eyes found the big ball in the sky; then it went black and soon it turned into a ball of metallic mercury and it kept moving around. Then I saw it go through several color transformations until I felt my brain spark up and images started flashing before my eyes.

Tanner was yelling at me.

"Look down, Henry, look down!"

I looked away and everything went black; then slowly my vision corrected itself.

"How do you feel?"

"I feel lighter than air."

"Good, good."

"No fuck, I think I'm going to puke," and I did all over the bait that we had in a bucket at my feet.

# 14

My head kept swirling and I had to lie down. Soon, I fell asleep in his daughter's room. I dreamed about wild horses galloping around and bucking in great open fields until a wave of blood crashed in from a hidden shore, covering everything in sight. I woke up in a panic. I looked up and found a goddamned stuffed animal of a horse staring straight at me.

I walked out into the living room and found Tanner sitting in his medicine chair, listening to music and drawing something. He had his vision-quest glasses on and he couldn't see me.

I sat down.

"Tanner, I need a loan."

He popped the things out of his eyes and looked at me.

"Henry, what's the problem?"

"I'm behind. I'm not going to make it till August. I need something to hold me over."

"Look around, Henry."

I was sitting in his $12,000 Eames chair.

"I don't have much, but what I do have is from living within my means."

"I'm not looking for a lecture, Tanner."

"Listen, we have some recruits coming to school tomorrow for a workshop, and I'm supposed to give them a talk on "The Future of Architecture." If you're interested, I can arrange to have you paid for it, if you think you can do it."

"Sure, Tanner, I'll do it. I assume you already have it all laid out."

"Not exactly. I'm working on it right now."

I looked at what he had. It wasn't much.

"All right, hell. I'll go to the library and get something together tonight."

"Good man, and don't forget to come at it with an optimistic view. These are our recruits and we need to get them signed up by the end of the day tomorrow."


Once at the library, I hit the files with a merciless abandon. If they wanted a treatise on the state of architecture, I'd give it to them. We'd go back to the horror of the Industrial Revolution, then I'd drag them through the madness of so-called progress and planned obsolescence until they all vomited in their mouths and ran out of the place with hate in their eyes for everything associated with the word "architecture."

# 15

The auditorium was full to the gills with the tiniest of humans. They all gyrated in their seats like tadpoles just born out of a swamp as I shuffled through my papers.

I fired up the first slide.

"Does anyone here know what this is?"

Silence like a black hole sucked the life out of the room.

"This is the first recorded man-made structure, something we like to call 'architecture.'"

I followed up with many other examples of so-called "primitive" architecture, and was sure to point out how they were all not only built to persist, but to also negotiate within transitional zones in the landscape.

I pointed up to the screen.

"These people would have never dreamed of plopping a building down in the middle of prime agricultural land, something that is unfortunately still widely considered an acceptable practice."

I ended with a slide of the most recent addition to our campus, a housing complex built in the exact footprint of where a 400-year-old hospital had once stood.

"This hospital survived some of the most powerful earthquakes in recent history. Now, does anyone know the life expectancy for our new Residence Hall?"

Silence.

"20 years. Renovating the hospital was considered too expensive, so they bulldozed it."


It had gone on for an hour, and by the end, I was sweating profusely. Then there were questions from the audience.

"How much does an architect make a year?"

I looked down at my deck shoes. In the left one, I saw my big toe poke out of a hole.

"There's handsome allowances for the architect. They are as important as doctors in some countries."

"How about this one?"

"Good question." I felt my hands start to tremble.

"Listen, that's enough questions for now. The director wants some time to talk with you before you leave this afternoon."

I got out of there after climbing the hundred steps to the exit. Once in the hall, I beelined it to the office. The secretary was eating lunch at her desk.

"No credit yet. The system is down. We're waiting for a check from Brag's office. It'll be here after lunch."


I drove to Louie's and ordered a beer. The news was on: "MIRACLE HEART PATIENT AND FATHER GONE MISSING."

The bartender looked at me. "What's new?"

"Someone stole the Red Beast."

"No shit? You hear about the girl gone missing?"

I looked at him, "Sure. Everything is disappearing these days."

"Some people think it's the Cloud People fucking with us again. *Dateline* just had a special on last night saying that they're planning something big this year, like a whole takeover or something."

"Well, let them. Who cares? Maybe they have a better way of handling things than we do."

"Whoa now. We can't have that kind of talk in here, Henry. If we don't have our sovereignty, then what do we have?"

"Just hit me with another beer, will you."

I drank and waited and the news ran on, then I returned to the office and grabbed my check for the lecture and blew out of there for the closest check-cashing place. Finally, I had enough cash to last me a few days, and I wasn't going to let another minute slip by without trying to find my Camaro.

# 16

I went straight for the bastard. I drove the little car up the freeway to the Mark 5 headquarters. I found armed guards patrolling the gate.

"What's your business here?"

I looked around for an answer.

"You here for the photo shoot at Plant 9?"

"That's it."

He let me through. A photo shoot? Sure, why not?

There was a sea of cars in the lot. I had to park far out near the fence then walked through the heat toward the entrance.

Inside, it was cold. To my right, I found a woman with severe eyes and large breasts signing everyone in. We had to sign a waiver: nothing that took place there could be discussed with anyone or we'd be imprisoned indefinitely.

I was handed a nametag and a number and told to sit down in a large waiting room. I sat next to a man with shaky hands.

"You got busted, too?" he said.

I looked at him. I had no idea what he was talking about. Then it came out. He was a smalltime pornographer who got busted red-handed with a bunch of women tied up in his apartment. "You have no idea how much housewives will pay for my services."

Now he was summoned by the Mark 5 to work off his punishment, either that or serve hard time.

"They'll take us up in groups of three," he said. "One cameraman, one lighting guy, and whoever has the biggest cock will be on detail."

A skinny kid sat dosed out across from us. It was an interesting waiting-room experience to say the least.

When the woman called out our numbers, our little group rose and we made our way to the big table in the middle of the room. There were evaluations to conduct on us. It all promised to be very scientific.

We were expected to serve a weeklong sentence and would not be able to leave the premises till then. My first move toward revenge landed me in a jail sentence, good going.

Our rooms were all off of the same hall. No windows anywhere. It was like being in the bowels of a ship out to sea but without deck privileges.

The kid won the longest unit award after the physical, so I was to be the lighting man. At the first setup, the cameraman saw my confusion and walked me through it when no one was watching. No natural light had its advantages. No pipe and drape to worry about. No blocking out the sun. Instead, we dressed up a makeshift bedroom scene. The Mark 5 had flare for detail. The room looked like Natalie's, complete with the crap a high school girl would have laying around. The laser gun I had securely stuffed in my pants went undetected thus far, but how long until I got another pat-down, no one could tell. As I placed all the crap on the shelves, I snuck it out of my pants onto the shelf. It looked natural there among all the other junk and toys. In plain sight, my feeling was that no one would notice it.

Once I got the lighting rigs up, our man needed to check his camera settings, so I had to lie on the bed like I was about to get some. Strange business, this porn business. I struck a few poses for the hell of it, and just when I started getting comfortable, a woman was pushed through the door.

"Starting without me?" she said.

I stood up and straightened myself out.

"Sorry, baby. I'm just the lighting tech." I pointed to the kid.

"He's your man."

There was nothing shy about her; she was a pro and looked, if nothing else, bored. She was not nervous at all. This was just a new form of probation. Nothing more, nothing less.

She didn't waste any time dropping her robe and getting to work. Her skin was like warm cinnamon in the bright light of the room.

By the third round, the kid was given a rest and was replaced. Later, he told me he thought he'd get a break, but they just gave him a few injections and pushed him into a theater where he was forced to watch sex films that would prime him for the following rounds to come.

# 17

The next day, he told me he wouldn't be able to make it a week. He feared the worst. He'd either be dead or impotent for life when the week was done. "I can't feel anything anymore," he said, "I think they broke my penis."

I felt for him. No pubescent boy on earth would believe it, but it was true—all the fun can quickly run out of it if the circumstances were wrong.

A few days later, I was summoned to the task. The extra-large boys were dropping like flies, and it was time to break in the B-list. That was my group.

Before my big performance, they took special care to work on me a bit with the films and the injections because of my age. After all, there were punishments much worse than this, and I even started to strut around like a prizefighter in my robe as *go* time approached.

But there were delays. The next girl up was giving them a hard time, so I just found myself discussing politics with the crew while my dong stood at attention.

It was my first taste of show business, and I felt ready.

# 18

Now the kid was assigned to the lights. There was no envy in his eyes, but I had a technique I learned years before, something he knew nothing about. I knew I could hold just enough back to keep going on strong through the long three-day haul. I'd give up a little something but not everything; I'd have to save some life force for myself.

When the next girl was thrown in, she dashed onto the bed face down and started weeping. We all just stood there looking at each other. My dong was still pronounced, but wavering.

The constant action had started to work on us. Somehow we had forgotten our true reason for being there, and we had played along long enough to forget that we were all prisoners, responsible for inflecting horrible things upon trapped women.

At the thought of it, Johnny Dong went dead and I closed my robe tightly against my paunch. The Mark 5 could all go and fuck themselves, I thought. What we needed to do was revolt, but who knew what horrors lay ahead if we tried something like that. I looked up and saw the laser gun poking its nose out from behind an electric Teddy bear.

After I sat down on the bed, I touched the girl's shoulder. "Now, don't get weird. We're all in the same boat here. Nobody's going to do anything they don't want to. And you know what? This is my first time in this business. I was shaking like a leaf before you flew in here."

She sat up and looked at me. It was Natalie. Her hair had been dyed jet black. When she saw it was me, she threw her arms around my neck, and we held each other for a long time while the crew just stood there with their mouths open.

# 19

After a quick powwow, we found ourselves in the same situation we were in before. We were there to make porn, and if we didn't, well, no one had any idea what kind of hell that would bring. It was time to brainstorm.

"Well, honey, we could just go ahead and do it," I said.

Natalie hit me in the arm with a closed fist.

"All right then, what's the next move?"

"She could fake a seizure. Then we could grab a guard and steal his light stick and we could make a run for it," said the kid.

"What's today?" I asked.

Nobody had any idea.

"Hold on." I had cut into my leg with my fingernail every twenty-four hours, at least what I thought was every twenty-four hours. But after inspecting myself, I found only four marks. The others seemed to have healed. I couldn't tell.

"Who knows? Maybe today is our last day?" I said.

"Even if is, how does that help us?" asked the cameraman.

"Well, Natalie and I could go for hours if we have to. If we time things right, every time the squareheads come to fetch her, we can get back into it. They're not going to cut us short, will they?"

I pointed to the kid. "The first time you went at it, it went on forever, right? And they just left you alone knowing it was quality footage; they just walked away, didn't they?"

We all thought about it.

"But what happens to me when they take you all away? They'll just throw me in another room full of perverts."

"Listen, after a long haul like that, they'll have to let you rest. We'll get out of here legitimately, and then we'll circle back to the theater and free you. Just like that." I drew a circle on the bed sheet with my finger to emphasize my point.

"Hold on, partner"—the cameraman spoke up—"don't include us in your plans. When I see the light of day, I'm skipping out as fast as my feet will bring me."

I looked at the kid.

"I'll help you. The bastards got me for simple possession of nP13, and when they crashed into my place, my cat had a heart attack and dropped dead right there while she was eating her dinner. Maybe she choked. I'm not sure exactly. She just dropped like a sack of rice off of the countertop."

We all looked at the cameraman.

"Aw, hell. Why not? Let's take these fuckers down."

The mood in the room was bright, but my dong was missing in action. I walked up to the shelf and grabbed

Natalie's laser gun and flipped it in my hand like Jesse James.

"Remember this?"

"You have a weapon? Then why the fuck do we have to go through with all this other bullshit? Let's just grab one of the guards and get the fuck out of here?"

"Yeah," the others agreed, "why go through all that if you have a weapon? Let's just make a run for it."

I looked down at my honker, and he wasn't responding anyway. I was sure it had something to do with all the eyes in the room.

"Yeah, I meant to say that. I was thinking that we'll just get the fuck out of here now. That's what I meant to say."

# 20

We set up the scene quickly. I disrobed and got on top of Natalie while she held the gun on her belly. The potential violence in the room sent a spark of lust into my heart and my soldier stood up. Natalie looked at me, then grabbed it in her hand. "There'll be plenty of time for that later, Henry."

"Promise?"

I leaned forward and kissed her as the guards crashed in through the door waving light sticks around, and they wanted to know what was taking so long. I started thrusting.

"Can't you bums see that I'm working here?" I said; then the damn thing found its way in, and Natalie let out a gasp. On the third thrust it was like diamonds were forming in my brain. God was real. We started going at it in earnest and the walls caved in. Thoughts of her thighs wrapped around my head came back to me, and it was too much. I pulled out and started shooting it everywhere just as Natalie pushed me off of the bed onto the floor. From my snail's eye point of view, and in my exasperated state, I witnessed Natalie take aim and shoot both of the squareheads in the face with the unmatched speed and grace of a cheetah. They both fell to the floor, paralyzed.

Natalie stood up, put on her robe, and crossed the room. From my spot on the ground next to the bed, she appeared to be a hundred feet tall, and all legs. She picked up my jeans and threw them at my head. "Get up, old man. We have business to attend to."

It was just like *Star Wars*, but nobody knew what the hell that was, so I didn't bother saying it. The cameraman and the kid put on the guard's uniforms and grabbed their light sticks, then herded us out into the hall.

Very soon the smell of shit would fill the room. I was sure of that.

# 21

Neither the cameraman nor the kid had any wheels, so we had to pack into the ancient Geo Prizm like a gang of misfit clowns. Weighing it down, we got out of there without incident, but we were surely marked from that moment on. Once we hit the freeway, we cruised at a steady 45 mph.

I stared at the rearview while my foot slammed the pedal down to the floor. As we putted along, I was sure at any second the bastards would appear behind us, but they didn't. There was nothing approaching us but idle lunch commuters and old couples taking a leisurely joyride. As we all leaned forward, we watched them pass us with ease.

"Where in the hell are we going now?" the cameraman asked.

"I'll drop you wherever you want, but the missus and I are going to track down her father and find my Red Beast."

They didn't like that. I had gotten them into this mess and they didn't have any idea in hell of where to go.

"Jump on a bus and go to Neo Mexico," I said. "Lay low and ride it out."

The cameraman spoke up, "Easy for you to say, but I'm broke."

"Me too," said the kid.

"All right, you no good pimps. I'll do this for you. I have a little cash. I'll spot you for your travels."

The cameraman liked the idea. With all his equipment confiscated, he had no way to make ends meet, plus they'd be after him. Unlike us, he had a nervous disorder and knew he couldn't run on his own."

We dropped him off at the Greyhound terminal. I spotted him a few hundred then he boarded the bus. The kid wasn't interested in running. He wanted to take the bastards down. His eyes were filled with hate.

"All right, Bubba. All in good time. First we take care of our business, then you can do whatever it is you feel you need to do."

Natalie tugged at my arm and looked up at me. "Let's go and find my father, Henry."

"Not yet, baby. Not just yet."

# 22

Fearing they had the make on the Geo, we drove to Betterton's place at the lake. Night had fallen and we could see him pacing around inside the house with his robe on. He was talking to himself with a martini in his left hand and a cigar in the other.

"He'll never give up his Roadster 5000," I said. "We'll have to steal it."

"Then he'll just report it."

"Not Betterton. He hates cops with a passion. He takes matters into his own hands. He'll try to track us down through his own methods, which in the end could be worse, but it'll give us enough time to let him know what took place. He says it all the time: 'Don't ever ask for permission. Only ask for forgiveness when the time is right.' Besides when he finds the Geo, he'll put it all together."

We waited for the lights to go out, then approached the roadster and I realized I had no idea how to steal a car.

"Leave this to me," the kid said.

The kid pushed me out of the way and went to work. In no time he had the thing open without any alarms blaring. He jumped in the driver's seat and started fucking with wires until it turned over.

"Good job, you little son of a bitch."

Then a shot rung out and the kid's head exploded, and he slumped over dead. Blood was all over the passenger's seat. I pushed the kid across the console and jumped in while Natalie dove head first into the backseat. Betterton was still yelling and shooting wildly at us as we tore through the wooded path towards the light of the road.

# 23

Now we had a dead kid on our hands.

"Jesus Christ."

Natalie was screaming into the seat as I drove 10 over the limit. I kept stopping myself from pushing it too hard even though the roadster could hit 250 mph in a straightaway.

"Where are we going?

I took the first exit. "We're going back."

"Where?"

"We're going back to Betterton's place."

"Why?"

"He won't, under any circumstances, call the cops. He'll find the body on his property and he'll dispose of it himself; that'll get this problem out of our hands."

All the lights were off at the house when we approached the drive. Our lights were off, too, and just when we were in the trees, I got out and laid the kid out onto the ground.

"We can't just leave him here."

"Trust me, this is better than the second option."

"And what was the second option?"

"Dropping him off at the city dump."

## 24

After picking up something for Natalie to wear, we made a quick stop at my place; then we drove for a few hours on pure adrenaline and plenty of EP14. When we found an isolated carwash, we rinsed out the car's interior. Not far off was a small roadside motel. We parked in the back and checked in as Mr. and Mrs. Stanley Kubrick.

The room was cheap and smelled like asparagus. We took our bags up the open-air stairs and Natalie showered. I went and got some ice from the machine. When I returned to the room, she was still in the shower, so I walked across the parking lot to the fueling station. There was a fence blocking the way, so I had to jump over it.

Inside, I picked out some chips, some juice, some candy bars, and some beers. The man behind the counter was talking with a girl with mascara caked eyes. She was drinking something out of a large styrofoam cup, and she watched me closely as I paid.

"Is there another way back to the motel?" I asked him.

"Yeah, you got to go around. If you fall and break your neck, maybe you try to sue. If I were you, I wouldn't jump it again."

"Okay," I said.

Outside, I walked for a while but didn't see an opening. Then I noticed that the guy and the girl came out and were either watching me or actually dumping the ice from the coolers. I waited till they went back inside before I jumped the fence again, this time catching my pant leg on my way down and I fell forward, hitting my head on the ground with my leg still stuck up there.

They ran up to me.

"You stupid asshole. I told you not to do that. You see what happens to stupid people?"

It was a mess. The bag of chips was open and had scattered all over the place. Some of the beer from a broken bottle ran toward me and soaked my shirt and hair.

The man took a big knife out of his pocket and cut me loose.

"Next time you try that I'll kick your ass."

I stood up and dusted myself off and the girl looked at me with contempt.

"Whatever happened to the rights of the pedestrian? The man on foot who was at one time free to roam the land?"

"That's not my concern, mister. I'm only interested in keeping people from jumping this fence."

I had the laser gun in my pants and I could have crapped them both out in a flash but decided against it. There was no sense in bringing any attention to myself.

After Natalie put ice on my head, we couldn't sleep so we kept the oxygen screen burning all night long just for the company. In the morning I'd call Betterton. Let him clear out the body tonight and get some rest. If I caught him before 8:00 a.m., we could sidestep all the confusion.

We found a channel with nothing on but a constant flow of clips from burning lava and volcanoes erupting around the world. We kept it there as the room filled with a soft red-orange light.

We were alone, but it wasn't a happy time. God only knew what kind of horrors were being inflicted on her father as we lay there together in the uncomfortable bed, and I knew that we would have to find him soon if there would be any chance of getting him out alive.

# 25

In the morning I got Betterton on the horn.

"You fucking maniac," he said, "I almost killed you."

"What can I say? It's been a weird few days."

His voice was not friendly. "All right, let me call off my guys. Jesus, I just slammed down five grand for your ass."

I gave him the guarantee that if anything happened to the roadster, I'd give him my Camaro to replace it.

"Yeah, that's if you can ever find it. It's probably in Baltimore by now anyway."

"Why Baltimore?"

"It's a long shot, but I know some guys, and they're always talking about driving hot stuff up there. It's supposedly some kind of Mecca these days for burnt items."

"Well, I have a hard time believing anyone would just sell it off like that," I said. My feeling was that the goons took it to the Chinaman, and he had it locked up in a garage somewhere like a trophy.

"Suit yourself. But my money is on Baltimore. Northward bound is rightward bound."

# 26

We drove to a diner for breakfast. Eggs, grits, reishi mushroom tea, strong coffee, and astralagus pancakes.

Betterton said he would report the Geo stolen and keep it hidden in the woods till the shit cleared. That would keep them from tracing the roadster. "You owe me, goddamn it," he said. "I never ever call the cops, so for this you're going to pay, and don't forget it."

Luckily, we had kept our hands on the two uniforms, but neither fit us, so we'd have to make some alterations. Natalie had everything she needed back at her father's house to do the job. She'd been living with him ever since going back to school. She was an architecture student now, but she had been into fashion before and knew how to put clothing together. We quickly grabbed her portable sewing machine kit, then stopped at a fabric store to aid in replicating the guard's shirt, for my paunch area especially. It was shameful, but it had to be done. If we ventured back into the Mark 5 headquarters and tried to track down her father, we'd need to go in as guards. We couldn't think of any other way.

Back in our motel room, Natalie worked and I drank beer and danced around the room. I was trying to seduce her. I put on a show and removed my Hawaiian shirt slowly. Occasionally, she would hand me a piece of fabric, and I'd get to work with the scissors, but it wasn't working out that well. Finally, she got annoyed with me and kicked me out of the room. I walked down to the lobby and sat on an oversized couch. The news was on and I pulled at a beer. CLOUD PEOPLE DETERMINED TO ATTACK was the headline of the day.

I looked at the kid behind the front desk?

"You ready for the apocalypse, son?"

He just grinned knowingly and I walked up to him.

"What do you have behind that counter?"

He looked around, then brought up a Krinkov machine gun.

"Where the fuck did you find that?"

"Ex-military. I have a 2C:58-5 license to protect and serve if all hell breaks loose."

"Nice. What's your name?"

"Lieutenant Johnny T. Vollmann."

"Well, Lieutenant, what else do you have behind that counter?"

"Nothing else here, but I have an arsenal lining the walls of my trailer."

I explained my situation to him. Told him we were also agents but deep undercover with specific details of the approaching invasion.

His green eyes sparked up. He had been prepping for it since he first learned of the phantoms in the sky. Their children, on one of their training missions, had taken out a hospital building on South First, where his mother was a nurse. One hundred thirty-eight killed in the explosion, including his mother.

"Listen, we're so underground that we've been temporarily cut off from our funding source. We've been listed as MIA. There can be no link, you understand?"

His eyes told me he understood, and he promised to swing back to our room in the morning with two high-powered stunners that would be easy to conceal. Then he asked to come with us, but I told him I couldn't make any promises. We shook hands and he said that he would be ready if needed.

# 27

Next morning, I put on the uniform and walked around the room. The name on my uniform said "Chinaski."

"Hey, don't fuck with me, I'm Chinaski," I said. I liked the sound of the name.

Natalie's grey fatigues were perfectly tailored, and I watched her heart-shaped ass cross the room. "Baby, you'll kill them with your walk alone."

But she was in a serious mood, especially this morning, and she just stared at me. There had been no romance since the porn shoot. My powers were wavering to say the least.

At 8:00 a.m. Johnny from the front desk knocked and we asked for a password. I saw him chew his lip through the peephole.

"There isn't one."

"Good answer."

I let him in. He saw us in our gear and started pacing around the room.

"If you're going to infiltrate the Mark 5, you have to take me with you. Those bastards have been involved with the Clouds from the beginning."

He had a black duffle bag with him, and he flung the thing onto the bed and opened it.

"These stunners are useful when dealing with Clouds, but you'll need more if you're taking down the Mark 5. I've got bead tranquilizers and Mafia bombs and GR15s the size of a package of cigarettes. You can't go in there unprepared."

Natalie looked at me then spoke up: "Do you know anything about the layout of the place? Can you get us to the Chinaman?"

His face went white. "That's no Chinaman; he's a Cloud. Don't you people read the files?"

He looked like he was going to start pulling his hair out with frustration as he kept walking around the room.

"All right, Bubba, let us get your measurements. Then, we'll go and pick up what we're missing from your place."

He looked at Natalie with dreamy eyes and said, "You won't regret this. I'm a veteran, and I'll defend our sovereignty with my last breath if necessary."

I grabbed him by the shoulders and moved him toward Natalie as she sat down on the bed and began opening her sewing kit.

# 28

After I changed into my jeans, we left Natalie in the room to get to work on the soldier's uniform and we took the Roadster 5000 to his place. The trailer was parked illegally and hooked up in the back of a machine shop. He knew the owners and had worked out a deal. His sewage drained out into a nearby ditch.

Inside, he typed a code into a panel and an entire wall lifted on hydraulics. When the high-powered lights popped on, his equipment shone like a display at a museum. I was impressed but didn't want to show it.

"Hurry up, Bubba."

"Hold on just one second. I have to show you this first." He took out a canister, "Any idea what this is?"

"Don't insult my intelligence."

"All right then, show me how you use it."

He handed me what looked like a metallic egg.

"Go ahead."

"Listen, kid, we don't have time to."

Just then, the thing blew up in my hand. It didn't do much of anything. It just shot out a thick cloud of white smoke that quickly filled the trailer. It smelled like kind bud and tasted like Thin Mint Girl Scout Cookies.

The kid was laughing. "It's a marijuana bomb. Throw this baby in a room and everyone will be stoned out of their minds."

"Jesus." I tried not to breathe it in but couldn't help it, and we sucked some in for the hell of it, until he grabbed me and we ran out of there. When we got to the car, I stood there leaning against the hood. I looked up at the sky. "Jesus, look at the fucking sky. Have you ever seen blue like that?"

"You're stoned."

"No, I'm not. I'm fine."

We started laughing, and we laughed for a while, standing there like a couple of maniacs until I got behind the wheel and the kid jumped in.

"Now, just shut the hell up and let me drive."

He was laughing like a hyena now.

"Shut up," I said. "We need music. I need something to take the edge off."

I crossed the ignition wires and flipped through the radio channels, but nothing worth a damn was on. News was poison. What we needed was something smooth, something to help ease the atmosphere for the drive. Finally, I found the songs of the ancients and I turned it all the way up. "Sympathy for the Devil" was just what we needed as we ventured off into the big unknown.

# 29

After we dressed, we loaded up and took off. The sky was still a full-blown ocean hovering just inches away from our heads.

"What's the deal with you two?" Natalie asked as we drove.

I looked at her.

"You two are stoned."

"No, we're not," I said.

"Then why are your eyes so red?"

"Allergic reaction."

She looked back at Johnny, who was grinning like a deranged monkey still.

"What the fuck?"

"It was an accident. Show her, Lieutenant."

He lifted a canister into his hand to show her, but the goddamned thing went off again.

"Holy fuck." We were coasting at a steady 45 mph, but I lost control anyway, and we ran off the road and hit the barrier.

The kid just sat there with the thing in his hand, and the car filled with white smoke until I couldn't even see him anymore.

"Throw it out of the window!" I yelled.

We all jumped out and he tossed it on the ground.

"Fuck that," I said. "Throw it further than that."

I looked at the damage. The front fender was smashed in, but the wheel would still be able to turn if only minimally. Along the passenger's side, dents and scratches reached across both doors. Everything seemed okay otherwise.

"Fucking Christ."

We jumped back in and rolled down the windows.

"Listen, Johnny, if you touch one more of those things, I'll beat you into a pulp."

He just sat there grinning. Nothing I said made any kind of impression on him and Natalie started laughing like it was the funniest thing in the world.

# 30

The closer we got to the Mark 5 headquarters, the tenser the atmosphere became. We'd have to get into character, but with so many goddamned unknowns that lay before us, the fear began to creep up on us all.

Instead of driving up to the gate, I took a sharp turn, grinding the tire against the fender, and we parked in a parking lot facing the gate from across the street.

"What are we doing?" asked the kid.

"We're observing."

We sat there for a long while and nothing happened.

"Maybe Johnny should get back into his jeans and we can bring him in as a prisoner," Natalie said.

I thought it over as a few guards approached in a van, waved to the guards at the gate, and made a little small talk.

"What if they all know each other?" Natalie said.

"That's not what bothers me. We didn't see any women guards enter or walking around when we were inside. We'll have to call the Better Business Bureau and report the sexist bastards," I said.

"What are you saying?"

"Honey, it's your choice; either sit back here or come in as a prisoner."

"And be forced into porn again? Forget it."

"Your call."

The kid looked at us. "Didn't they brief you? How can you not know there're no female guards until now?"

"Because we're not secret agents," Natalie said.

The kid pouted.

"It's true, Bubba. We're on the run. We're just a couple of low-rent hustlers."

"Well then, that puts me in charge. I'm the only one here with any kind of military credentials."

I looked at him through the rearview.

"That may be true, but I'm old enough to be your great-great-great grandfather, and I'm not taking any orders from your little scrawny ass."

"Can I at least make a suggestion?"

"Shoot."

The kid's plan sounded good. He'd go in and see how everything operated and then he'd call us with instructions. We'd just sit tight until the call came. Simple enough.

He jumped out, crossed the street, and made it to the gate. He talked with guards for a second and we saw his hands moving as he explained his situation. He was going to tell them that he'd been in a car accident and that he had amnesia, which would help him out if he made any mistakes.

An hour went by until the call came.

"I was checked into a hospital unit. I'm in room 390C. I saw many people being booked and sent in for examinations. No one asked for anything from the guards, only the prisoners' names. Personnel will take her from there, and it looked like all the guards headed to an Education Wing. It's all clearly marked."

I looked at Natalie.

"It's your choice, baby."

"Are you kidding? My fucking dad is in there, and I'm going to find him." She pulled on a cigarette then said, "And if any sleazeball tries to put their thing into me, I swear I'll tie it into a goddamned knot."

She changed into a white sundress, then lifted it up and stuck a marijuana bomb into her polka-dotted panties. Good girl.

# 31

Because I was the officer that brought her in, I was handed a disc that would start flashing a red light when it was time to retrieve her. First, they'd clean her up, and then they'd run a series of tests on her.

I couldn't fit the thing into my pocket because I already had so many weapons in them. I just held onto it and headed for the Education Wing, but found that it wasn't an Education Wing at all. The room looked like the Gold Room from *The Shining*. I walked around and found an empty overstuffed chair and fell into it just as a white-coated waiter pranced up to me and took my order. His hair was slicked back like a baby seal.

"Scotch and soda," I said, "and how about some peanuts?"

I observed the goings-on in the room. This gig was better than any adjunct position. This was nothing less than a country club complete with all the perks. Just off the bar was the entrance to a spa. And just beyond that, an entrance to a cinema where a line was quickly forming. Once I got my drink, I grabbed the dish of peanuts and headed for the line.

# 32

I dropped peanuts everywhere when I sat down and one of the marijuana bombs in my pocket fell out and began rolling down to the front for what felt like an eternity. When it finally popped and went off, I could see the smoke rise from up front, but the film had started, and nobody said anything.

Here was nothing less than the screening room for all the crap being made in the place. It was a sad thing to see all the prisoners being forced to fuck like that. Some went at it with enthusiasm, but most were horror-stricken. It was lame bullshit. The only thing that makes porn worth watching is when the actors can convince the audience that they are enjoying themselves. Otherwise it's pure *horrorshow*.

In the end, the bomb didn't make much difference unless you happened to be sitting up front because most everyone in the place was smoking cigars.

Then, it happened.

Our shoot came onto the screen and I watched my own bigger than life lily-white ass going up and down. Following that, the whole escape scene unfolded and a special report was made. Anyone that brought us in would receive a vacation to the destination of their choice and a new car—my car. There it was. A still image of my Red Beast in all its glory, being whored off to the first pimp to successfully bring me in.

# 33

I didn't waste any time getting the fuck out of there before the lights came on. When I found the right door in the hospital unit, I knocked lightly and waited for a signal.

Inside the room, I looked down at Johnny. "Where can I find the Chinaman?"

He sat up and pointed. The bastard was sitting down in a chair with his three goons standing behind him.

"Good afternoon, Mr. Fields."

I drew the laser gun by mistake and fired. It went right through the bastard, and a goon standing behind him fell to the ground.

"No need for violence, my friend."

The fucker was a Cloud, and only the stunner would have done anything at all to him. When I went for it, the other two linebackers grabbed me.

"Now, don't you worry, Mr. Fields. We have a special place for your kind. Just wait and see. I promise you'll love it where we're taking you."

# 34

I was stripped of my hardware and taken to an auditorium and fastened into a seat.

We were all there: Natalie, her dad, the kid, and myself. Our eyes were held open with vision-quest goggles, and we waited for god knows what.

When gaffers and techs appeared on the stage, they started dressing the scene. What kind of spectacle lay ahead, we could only guess. Whatever it was, it was going to be sinister. I was sure of that. I couldn't turn my head at all but yelled out anyway, "Natalie, is that you?"

The voice came from my right side. "It's her father."

"Oh, I'm sorry about all of this, sir."

"Just remind me to hit you in the groin with my cane when we finally get out of this mess."

"Sure thing."

When the stage was lit up, a few ladies waltzed out from behind a curtain. There was a brunette in a blue blazer and a blonde in a red one. They were separated from us by a sheet of glass that ran the length of the stage. On our side, there were several speakers set up, so we'd be sure to hear whatever it was that was going to take place. I imagined horrible things, like they were going to start castrating gorillas on the stage.

As the show began, I quickly saw that it wasn't going to be anything like that. It was worse; it was a live recording of the Home Shopping Network. Item after item was brought in, and we suffered through every detail. Every time a new useless thing was brought up, I felt the increasing need to vomit. It went on like that for hours. Maybe it was a whole day. By the end of it, I felt like I was made of jelly, and my brain had retreated and gone into shock. I was numb from the waist down. When it was finally over, they had to lift me onto a gurney and wheel me out of there. As for the others, I had no idea where they were sent, and I feared the worst for Natalie.

# 35

Later, I awoke in a white hospital room just like the kid's. I was hooked up to tubes and machines, and my mouth was taped shut and my arms were bound at my sides.

There was an oxygen screen hanging on the wall and ancient episodes of daytime talk shows were running on a loop. Another form of torture. Dig deep, I thought to myself; you can beat this thing, don't lose it. Just hang in there.

I felt my teeth cringe when a nurse walked in the room. She had a face like a Greek statue and was as white as the walls. She wasn't human. Maybe she was a Cloud, a Cloud with an hourglass figure. I felt the lust burn in my groin. Blessed are the saints and all of their friends, I thought as I tried to speak to her, but she didn't respond to my grunts. Nothing. She just adjusted the controls on the machines and vanished out of the room after cutting the light and the screen off.

In the darkness, I laid awake and felt the stuff move through my blood. It didn't feel right. It felt acidic. I was sure I was being poisoned, and I'd be dead in the morning.

That night, I slept hard, and in the morning I awoke with faint memories and messages from my dream. The ghosts who had visited me before at my house had appeared to me, and they were still looking for favors. They'd help free me if I would agree to help take down the Clouds. I remembered agreeing to their conditions, but it wasn't fair. I was out of my mind, and they knew it. All I could do was wait and see if any of it was real. In my condition, I had no idea what the hell was going on.

# 36

It turned out to all be bullshit.

I just laid in the room for what felt like a week, maybe it was two. I had no idea. Without any hope of escaping, I felt the inevitable tide of depression begin to rise within me. My only distraction came from the angelic nurse who waltzed in from time to time with meals and injections until one day she came in with all the ghost-like turkeys I had seen in my place before. She removed the tape from my mouth and they explained it all to me.

"She's one of us, Henry, and she has been sneaking small amounts of EP14 into your system on a daily basis. We were here all along, but it is only now that you can see any of us."

"Great," I said. "Now, get me out of here."

"Not so fast. If we do that, everything will go to waste."

"But what about my team? I've got friends locked up in this joint. And what about my fucking Camaro?"

"We've already got your friends out safely, we assure you. They'll be waiting for you as soon as you help us. We didn't know about the car, but we'll get someone on that in due time."

"How do I know that any of this is true?"

"We have our ways, Henry. That is all I can say at this time."

He had something in his hand.

"Does this look familiar?"

It was Natalie's white and baby-blue polka-dotted panties that tied up on the sides like a string bikini. I looked at them.

"Hey, why the fuck do you have those?"

"Simple. It was all she had to give up that could identify her. She wanted me to give them to you."

He hung them over my face so I could get a good look.

"All right, you little creep. What is it exactly that you want me to do?"

I could see right through him as he stood there laughing. When he spoke, his little crackly voice filled the room. I didn't like him at all, but he had me by the balls and there was nothing I could do but listen to him.

# 37

How they managed to get me out of there, I had no idea. They did it during the night, and I assume I was heavily medicated. Next thing I knew, I awoke in the Roadster 5000 with my head leaning against the steering wheel. Drool was hanging from my mouth and making a stain on my jeans. The morning sunlight came in, and the colors from my Hawaiian shirt spread out into the car's interior. I felt hung over like a teenager after crashing his first wedding reception.

I turned the engine and spotted my .45 sitting in its holster on the passenger's seat. In the strong sunlight, I could see the blood we had missed while cleaning up the car that night. Dried black blood droplets were still spread out across the passenger's side window. If you looked carefully, you could see sand-like bone fragments from the poor kid's skull stuck to the interior of the passenger door. This was turning out to be one truly fucked summer.

Next to the gun, there was a notebook full of instructions. I flipped through it, but there were so many of them that I'd have to find a place to sit and read through them carefully. Once I got into a booth at a roadside diner, I began to read and it was like reading a dissertation full of historical justifications for this and that. I skipped most of it and finally found the chapter entitled "Operations for a Free World."

I could feel my eyes glazing over as I read. It was like reading the instruction manual for putting together a microwave oven from scratch. As my eyes moved across the page, I finally hit something I could understand. Movement #33: Find Stanley McCormic.

Whatever Stanley had been gibbering about the last time I saw him at the Black Garter must have been true, because they cited him as the only human to successfully return from their limbo world. Stanley was the only one to crack the code, and it was now my job to get his secret and deliver it to them in exchange for my friends and my car. I lit a cigar and sat there with my head still aching. When the waitress came by to refill my coffee, I stopped her and ordered a double Bloody Mary on ice then sat back and waited for it for what felt like an hour.

# 38

It was nearly 8:00 a.m. and Stanley wouldn't be at the Black
Garter till at least 9:30. I had an hour and a half to regroup
before tracking him down.

The first thing I needed to do was change clothes and
dump the roadster. Driving around in that thing was like
driving a Mardi Gras float through Rome during Lent as far
as I was concerned. No, the roadster would have to be left
behind.

I decided to take the bastard to the airport. Maybe it
would look like I flew to Afghanistan or any other major
vacation destination these days, which wouldn't hurt my
situation.

After sneaking the Bloody Mary out of the diner with the
help of a newspaper, I maneuvered through the early-

morning congestion with the drink jammed between my legs.

In the end, I decided to leave the roadster in the far corner of the LAX parking lot, facing the freeway. In bold letters I wrote out *$500 or Best Offer* on a piece of paper with a marker, then fastened it inside the windshield. Underneath, I wrote Betterton's phone number. He'd have it back in a few hours if all went well.

Inside the notebook, I found several large bills. There were plenty enough there to buy myself a new getup and rent some new wheels, and then if the shit got heavy, I could fly anywhere in the world first class if I played my cards right.

In fifteen minutes, I drove away from the airport with a classic fully automatic white Coupe de Ville. The boy at the counter said that the owner had bought it in Las Vegas and that it had been in many movies from the late twentieth century: "This is the exact car Depp drove in *Fear and Loathing*."

I looked at him.

"Don't mean a goddamn thing to me, friend. I'm in show-business myself, and I can tell you it's no goddamn picnic, you hear me? And don't you ever forget it. Steer clear. Stick with the gig you have now. In fifty years, you'll be manager, and in seventy-five, you'll be the owner. Think about it."

What in the hell was wrong with me? I was sweating like a pot roast in an oven as I drove out of there. After jumping a curb, I reached for the knobs and the buttons and banged on them with my fist until the cool air shot out of the thing into my face. At the freeway, I cut the wheel and gunned the bastard to the nearest clothing store and prepared myself for whatever the hell was coming next.

# 39

I didn't pay any attention to what kind of clothing store I had driven up to. When I walked through the swinging doors, I suddenly saw it all laid out clearly before me. I had walked into *Cal's Country and Western Store and Saloon established circa 1959.*

Row upon row of cowboy boots shone in the dim light of the place in every color imaginable. I took a black pair of Larry Mahan's off the shelf and put them on with some difficulty. In my fucked-up jeans, they looked cartoonish on my feet, but when I found a black suit and cowboy hat, they turned out to be just right. After that, I found a belt with a silver bull skull for a buckle. If this was going to be my last ride, I was determined to go down in the right attire, no matter what.

The ride to the Black Garter was uneventful aside from a random asteroid tearing ass across the sky and crashing into the Pacific Ocean to my right. "Jesus fucked Mary," I said as I watched the thing burn across the sky. If the Cloud Invasion had already begun, how could they be stupid enough to shoot into the ocean?

After convincing myself that it was just a random asteroid, I found a parking spot in the rear of the Black Garter near the fire exit. Taking my time, I positioned the thing nose out and ass in, and I made sure to leave the engine running. It was something the dead kid had taught me. I grabbed my .45 and strapped it on.

Stanley was there like every morning, but he ignored me when I sat down and ordered a beer. My stomach was ill at ease and I didn't want to risk the repercussions by drinking anything harder.

In the cowboy getup, no one recognized me, including the bartender. As far as they were concerned, I was just another blue blood from Dallas coming out West to go on a honky-tonk.

I had every intention of explaining my situation to them, but when I began swallowing my first hit of beer, a goon appeared through the door and shot the bartender deader than a roast beef sandwich. As far as I knew, Stanley was dead too.

When the noise started, I spit out the beer, ninja rolled onto my shoulder, then squatted with the .45 centered at the goon's sternum and fired. A ball of fat hit the wall behind him. A head is easy to miss, but a torso is like hitting a billboard.

What followed was severe moaning and groaning coming from the goon, and I knew that I'd have to shoot the bastard again, and that was a completely different story. It was an ugly situation already, and now I'd have to walk up to him and finish him off like a Nazi.

"Why the fuck did you have to do this?" I asked him. "Now, I have to fucking execute you, you son of a bitch."

His gun was still in his hand, and when I sensed movement, I popped him in the head twice then ran for Stanley, who was lying flat on the ground. His head was on the footrest, and he was choking on blood that came out of his mouth like chocolate syrup in the dim light.

I shook him by the shoulders.

"What is it, Stanley? What is the goddamned secret?"

He just opened his right hand, and with his thumb, he pointed to his Super Bowl ring. That's all he did. I had no idea what the fuck it meant. I shook him again and said, "Come on, you bastard, tell me what that means?"

He was unresponsive. I looked around the place. Burnt gunpowder and the stench of human blood filled the room.

I grabbed his blood-covered ring finger in my hand, but the ring wouldn't budge. The goddamned thing was glued to his fat finger.

I looked at his dead face.

"Sorry, Stanley, but it doesn't look like you'll be using this anytime soon."

I took his finger and placed the nose of my .45 up against it and blew it away into a thousand pieces. It took me five minutes to find the ring on the ground before I could run out the back and into the sun that hit me like a spotlight at a prizefight.

# 40

I refused to believe that the ring was just a useless and very expensive relic as I flew down the freeway with the top down toward Las Vegas. I'd been instructed to go there once I gained certain information, and as far as I was concerned, the ring had everything to do with the secret they were looking for. There was no other way to interpret the footloose dance that I'd been on.

In the open desert, I saw many more asteroids crashing onto the earth, and soon, a dust storm would rise and force me to stop and seal up the car. Before long, I was driving along at a crawl. At most, I could see twenty feet ahead of me. I decided to have a little conference with myself: "If there's any justice left in this world, then there's no reason in hell I can't floor this beast in a straightaway."

It was an idea worth contemplating, because if a sudden turn were to appear, I'd be stuck out several hundred yards into cactus in a matter of seconds without a hope in hell of getting out.

My cowboy hat hit the ceiling of the car and flew into the backseat when I floored the gas pedal. Fuck it, I thought. With my right foot hammered down to the ground, I took my hands off the wheel, grabbed the hat, and put it back on my head.

Only when I hit a rock in the road did I grab the wheel with both hands and force it to straighten out as I blasted into the limitless abyss ahead.

# 41

After half an hour of pure horrid driving conditions, I drove out of the storm and saw the lights of Las Vegas glowing in the distance. No one else on the road seemed to have come from where I had been. All the cars here were clean and shining in the afternoon sunlight like they'd just been driven off of a car lot.

When a big black LTD approached from the right lane, the driver peered at me through mirrored sunglasses. A woman's head in his lap went up and down with a feathered cowboy hat on. Dust had been floating up from the Coupe de Ville for the last 10 minutes, and now it was making its way into this man's open window. He lifted his fist into the air and began yelling at me.

"Oh, enjoy your blowjob and shut the hell up," I said as I hit the breaks, cut the wheel, then disappeared into a cross street.

There was a room waiting for me at the Coco-Lounge. I was to check in under the name "Burt Reynolds," but I had already decided that wasn't going to happen. Not this time. I didn't want anyone knowing I was there till I found them first. I had already fallen into too many traps to risk that again, and if anything, I had the strange feeling that I was becoming a bit more sophisticated. Perhaps the car was responsible for distorting my self-image.

I drove past the valet and made it into the parking lot of the Flamingo and backed into a spot near an exit.

The lobby bar was full to the gills with cowboys from Texas and Idaho. The rodeo was in town and the media was everywhere, tracking down riders and interviewing them as the event approached. Perfect. I'd fit in just right. No one would take a second look at me, I was sure of it.

I studied the notebook and ordered a coffee. As I reached to pay the waiter, he caught a glimpse of the Super Bowl ring.

"Holly Shit! Are you Terry Blaine, Super Bowl MMCCLXXXVIII?"

I was wearing black-as-the-night wayfarer sunglasses.

"Sir, can I have your autograph?"

I was stumped. When he held out a postcard, I scribbled some nonsense onto it, then grabbed his coat and pulled him toward me. "Listen, bud, you didn't see me, you got that?"

"Of course. Whatever you say, sir."

Later, I saw the geek talking to his floor manager, who then slid across the floor toward me.

"Is there anything we can get for you, sir?"

Before I could say anything, the man flipped out a deck of passes out of his coat pocket.

"I understand you may already have accommodations, but we would be honored if you would consider one of our rooftop suites."

All I had to do was present the pass at the front desk and everything would be taken care of.

Things could have been worse. Now, I was going to be a retired football star in one of biggest hotels on the strip. Considering that my plan was to sneak away to the south end in a budget room, things could have been much, much worse. Plus, the cash was getting tight if I wanted to keep a little on the side in case an emergency departure was in order.

I took the notebook with all my instructions and found the front desk. Within minutes, I was staring out of the eightieth-floor window, watching the last glimmer of the sunset lift from the golden desert beyond.

# 42

After a shower, I lay down in the bed and examined the ring. What did it all mean? The diamonds on it looked evil and mysterious. If nothing else, it was worth about five million dollars, and it didn't take me long to start spending that kind of money in my mind. I could always take the Red Beast down through Juárez at midnight, and when the banditos on the border zeroed in, if the roar of the Big-block V8 didn't stop their hearts, I'd flip the nitro-switch and disappear into the night like a thief. Within hours I'd be eating fish tacos and drinking beer in a hammock.

As the news ran on the oxygen screen, I stared up at the ceiling. A few buildings in downtown Los Angeles were on fire. Authorities weren't sure if it was caused by an asteroid or not. Even if they had been pulled down with explosives in broad daylight, it would still take a few centuries for the real cause to surface. Nothing has changed, and nothing will when it comes to that kind of business. If you want theater, turn on the news.

I found the general-info channel that described all the events for the evening and saw that the kickoff for the rodeo was fast approaching at 8:00 p.m. Inside the notebook, I found a ticket. Not missing it was emphasized.

Then there was a sharp knock on the door.

"Room service."

I grabbed a towel and looked through the peeper. Two dirty-blondes stood side by side in fur coats. They looked classy and professional. Their Egyptian-style eye makeup was just right, and when I opened the door, I saw that their toenails were covered in diamond dust.

"I didn't order anything."

"Compliments of the house."

They walked in and pulled off my towel. For the next hour, I was going to be a retired NFL quarterback, and I decided that was much better than being Burt Reynolds held up at the Coco-Lounge. I reminded myself, once gain, that things could have been much worse.

# 43

It was going to be a busy night for the girls and there was no time for chitchat after the acrobatics. They took turns in the toilet, then took off to work on the rodeo crowd after buttoning each other up.

After another shower, I got an idea. On the oxygen screen, I drew up the files and found a photograph of Natalie on the School of Architecture's website. I called down to the front desk and had the thing printed up, then drove to the Coco-Lounge and walked in with it.

The woman behind the counter had seen Natalie earlier and said that she had left with a group of men. "She was with some rodeo riders."

It looked like they were having a party.

"Are you going to be in the rodeo this evening, honey?"

I felt like I had been in a rodeo for that last few weeks. "Sure, I'm running the barrels. I'm a world champion."

"Well, honey, you need to get going. It's already started."

I looked around the lobby. There were a few men in black suits reading the newspapers, an ancient practice for spooks.

As I walked outside, I decided that it was high time for something to start making sense. I was walking blind into an uncertain future, and doom hovered just beyond the horizon. I was sure of that.

When I pulled out of the lot, a black sedan quickly followed me. It was surely the suits from the lobby on my tail. I made a U-turn at Caesars Palace Drive, then gunned it and turned left onto East Flamingo Road. After a few quick right turns, I found the T&M Center and parked the beast ass in without anyone on my tail.

The T&M Center looked like a circus tent turned into a spaceship. In the parking lot, many people were arriving late and hitting Lightweight Travelers as they stumbled toward the massive stairs that led up to the entrance.

I didn't take the stairs; instead, I snaked around back to where the rough stock had been loaded in for the show. A few rodeo clowns were fighting, and security officers were trying to pull them apart when I managed to slip inside. Natalie was nowhere in sight, so I fell in line with a group of cowboys making their way toward the bucking chutes. As we approached, numbers were pinned on our backs. I kept moving ahead without an idea in hell of what I was doing there. The barrel race had just finished up, and the winners were being announced on the loudspeakers.

Soon, the bull riders would mount up. We inched along like cattle ourselves until the cowboy in front of me climbed the gate of the chute in order to drop down on a filthy black bull that had nothing less than pure hate in his eyes. I looked around for a way out of there and into the stands, but I was stuck.

When the gate crashed open, the bull's hooves tore into the dirt and flung it into the air and onto our heads. A few seconds later, the bull rider was hanging on for his life and two clowns started diving in front of the bull until it jumped into the air, throwing the kid off and onto the ground with a deep thump. When the bull came down again, it kicked and thrust its horns into the belly of one of the clowns. Blood was oozing out of the clown's mouth when he hit the ground in terror, and on the next jump, the beast trampled on the kid's femur and smashed it into two pieces. A weird second knee bent halfway up his thigh, and he screamed out in anguish as the clowns dashed in front of the bull again.

I turned around and started climbing the rails, but excited fans started screaming at me, "Go for it. You're next, buddy."

I had a good grip on the rails and pulled myself up, but a few cowgirls started stomping on my hands with their cowboy boots. I lost my grip and fell down onto the ground. After that, I was lifted up by a few other riders who led me to the chute, and before I knew it, I was seated on another bull that was sure to kill me in the next few seconds.

# 44

By the time the gate opened, my heart was banging around in my chest like a crazed wolverine caught in a cage. The thought of cracked femurs was the only thing that kept me on the thing as it leaped into the arena. On the second jump, the bull spun right, and my free hand swung around and hit my cheekbone, cutting my face with the Super Bowl ring.

After what felt like an eternity, I flew off the thing and hit the ground flat on my back. I couldn't breathe but managed to curl up into the fetal position. By the time they got me onto a stretcher, I was covered in mud.

Inside the locker room, it was quiet aside from the moaning coming from the other bull rider. The paramedics were trying to stabilize him for the ambulance ride to the hospital. I sat up and no one paid any attention to me. The room was cold and stunk of death. After managing to stand up, I dusted myself off, put on my hat, and walked out to a concession stand and ordered a beer.

The man behind the counter was talking to me while I searched for my wallet.

"You were number eighty-seven?"

I looked down.

"That was one hell of an ugly ride."

I could barely breathe and I didn't feel like talking. I just held myself up by clutching the countertop and drained half the beer. Soon, an arm found me and I was being hugged tightly. I felt my ribs burning up inside. A few were broken. I reached for the crazed fan's arms and started to push her away.

"Henry, it's me."

It was Natalie. She had on a cowboy hat and her hair was back to blonde.

"I liked you better as a brunette," I said.

"Where were you? We've been waiting for you."

"Where?"

"At the Coco-Lounge. You were supposed to meet us. We've been waiting."

"How was I supposed to know that?" I said as I put my hand on her waist and squeezed.

# 45

There was no time for small talk. The ghost was certain that, at any moment, the Clouds were going to begin their strike in earnest, and if we didn't act fast, we would all either be dead or worse—imprisoned indefinitely.

Natalie took a vial out of her pocket and dumped half an inch of it into my beer as we walked. "Here you go. Now let's get to the stands."

The show was still going strong. Cowgirls in rhinestone-studded shorts were standing on their ponies and whirling flags all in unison as fireworks started going off.

When we found our seats, the crew was all there, and when Natalie's father saw me, he said I didn't have to worry about the cane-to-the-crotch promise. After ass whipping like I had taken on the bull, he saw no need for it any longer.

I just sat down and drained the beer as the ghost started asking about the information he had been waiting for.

"Did you get it?"

I lifted my hand and waited for congratulations, but instead, the bastard started scolding me.

"What in the hell is that thing?"

"It's a Super Bowl ring. It belonged to Stanley."

"What did you ask him?"

"I asked him what the secret was, but he was bleeding to death and there wasn't much time for details. He just pointed to his ring with his thumb. So, I grabbed the thing and got the hell out of there."

The ghost held up his hand and tried out the gesture, but I corrected him.

"No, Stanley was wearing it on his right hand."

"You idiot, it wasn't about the ring. It makes a sixteen. We were looking for a number, and that's the number we need. It's the proper voltage for this device here." He pointed to what looked like a food processor from the mid-1980s that was sitting at our feet.

"Didn't you read the notebook we gave you?"

"Well, sort of." I was becoming annoyed with him. "Okay then, you no good pimp. I'll be keeping the ring then. How do you like that?"

He just stood up and skipped over to Johnny, who was sitting on the other side of Natalie.

"Now, wait just a goddamned minute," I said. "Where are my wheels? Me and the little lady have somewhere to go."

"Not so fast, Henry," Natalie said. "Any minute, the invasion is going to begin, and we are sitting at ground zero for a good reason. The Clouds have a thing for rodeos and pornography. They plan on swarming down on this place and holding us all hostage in a matter of minutes. The whole Mark 5 operation was an effort to curb an all-out invasion. All those Clouds are addicted to human porn. Can you believe it? It has something to do with the human form. Supposedly, they are all rectal-linear and not very sexy."

"Well, then, why the hell are we here? It doesn't make any goddamned sense. Shouldn't we be somewhere else where it's safe?"

Then, Johnny walked up and grabbed the thing at our feet and lifted it up.

"When they send their plasma beam down, we'll set the voltage on this thing and toss it into the beam's path. This will cause a chain reaction and destroy them for good."

"That sounds a little like bullshit to me, my friend," I said.

Natalie and the kid were standing close to each other now, and I noticed their knees touch a few times while they were sitting down earlier. Everything was getting weirder by the minute, and I needed a cigar.

"So, who's going to take this thing down there when the time comes?" I asked.

I looked around, but they were all looking at me.

"Jesus, I'm already a mess, and I don't think I have it in me."

I looked at Johnny. "I'm afraid you're the one with the proper credentials for this type of thing."

He thought about it. "You're right. I'll do it."

"But he can't," Natalie protested, "It's too dangerous."

"He's the one that said he would defend our sovereignty till his last breath. Sorry, kid, but those are your words."

He took Natalie's hand in his, "He's right, Natalie."

"But, we just got married."

I looked at her and her father said, "It's true. A lot has happened since you were gone, Henry. While we were all locked up, before the ghost freed us, we discovered that the only thing that would excuse Natalie from being forced into another porn shoot was being pregnant. The Mark 5 are sentimental in that way, and we were very lucky. Her test came back positive just in time."

"Jesus, how long was I locked up for?"

Natalie's father put his arm around his new son-in-law.

"You were gone almost a month. We thought you were dead. These two here, they were married just this morning. We even had a few of the rodeo riders with us as witnesses and for good luck. We had a nice crowd at the reception. You missed the whole thing, Henry."

"Aw, hell," I said. "I guess I was too old for you anyway, baby."

I felt my heart sink as I stood there looking into her blue eyes, but I knew it wasn't for any of the right reasons. I had used her as plaything when I could get away with it, and now that it was over, I couldn't help but feel happy for her. After I shook Johnny's hand, Natalie tilted back her cowboy hat and gave me one last kiss.

# 46

The rodeo went on for what felt like an hour after that, but in actuality, it only lasted about ten minutes before the roof crashed open, and a big blue pulsing beam from hell shot down into the center of the arena. When it came down, it hit a rider and turned him and his horse into dust instantly.

Everyone screamed and I jumped on a horse and rode out to the roaring hellish thing, but my timing was off, and when I tossed the clunky device the first time, it just dropped to the ground like a turd that had fallen out of a horse's ass.

"Fuck me!"

After that, I slid off the horse and grabbed the thing with both hands, then ran for the beam again and finally managed to get it into its path without being burned alive.

Within seconds, the beam started to convulse until red fire started climbing up it toward the opening in the roof. Many cowboys were still scattered around and running for the loose horses, but there were too many, and they started bucking like crazy in every direction imaginable. When I began running for it, ten paces from the gate, a giant mare passed close to me and knocked me on my ass.

Once up on my feet again, I ran another few yards until something else slammed into me from behind, and I hit the ground face first, and yes, O my brothers, it was a fresh pile of steaming horseshit that welcomed me, horizontal. Then, I saw the headline appear in my mind's eye: MAN SAVES THE WORLD FROM ALIEN INVASION AND FALLS FACE FIRST INTO PILE OF STEAMING HORSE SHIT.

And how it burned my eyes, O my brothers, but I got up and ran anyway, and your humble narrator made it into the deep bowels of the arena not because of the fear of death, but from humiliation. Pure and simple. A little humiliation can go a long way and can, when you need it most, provide just enough strength when the body has all but given up.

# 47

I was certain that the whole place was going to go up in flames at any second, but what did your humble narrator do? He disrobed and took a third shower of the evening deep in the bowels of the good ole T&M arena, and what an evening it was.

The place was nearly vacant when I walked out of there fresh from a cold shower, and as I approached the lonely Coupe de Ville in the O so lonely parking lot, I found a couple of mean-looking characters sitting on the hood of, none other than, my very own cherry-red Camaro SS 396. Yes, sir.

My body was fucked three ways from Sunday, but the sight of the Red Beast sent quivers up my spine, and my brain exploded like fireworks at the sight of it.

"I thought you only got the car after you got your man," I said.

"Well, cowboy, it looks to us like we do in fact got you."

I looked at them and saw only the green tint of a shadow run across both their faces.

"All it seems like to me is that a couple of evil gimps have their dirty asses smashed up against another man's car, so if either of you have any sense at all, you'll kindly remove yourselves from the Camaro."

Up in the sky, there was only a faint red light coming from where the beam had shot down.

"The war is over, friends. The geeks are finished, and a new era is upon us. There's no need for violence here."

They looked at each other and laughed.

"Maybe the war is over for you, but for us, it's just beginning."

"How's that?"

"We aren't Mark 5 men. We're infiltrators. We're Clouds. And your weapons won't work on us, Mr. Fields. The operation here was one of many. Most major cities across this planet are now in our control."

I had the .45 out and level with their heads. "So, you don't mind if I scratch your noses with this thing?"

The slug shot straight through one of the bastard's heads just as I finished squeezing the trigger. A second later, it skipped down the empty parking lot with a bleeding orange-pink spark.

Now, they were both falling over laughing like schoolyard bullies, and the idea of being completely fucked entered into my mind as I felt the Super Bowl ring on my finger. It was worth more than life itself. I was certain of that.

"You have any idea what this is?" I said as I tossed it toward one of them. "It can buy a lot of shit on this planet. I say it's worth a trade for my freedom."

The goon that caught the ring was inspecting it with care when a blue light suddenly shot out of the thing and into his eyes. For a brief moment after that, his face held a mesmerized gaze. Then slowly, at first, his face began to melt. Within seconds, the gradual drip turned into a full on gush of liquefied flesh as if a water balloon burst into a puddle of goop at his feet.

When the ring fell out of his dead hand (he had remained standing for a moment) I dove for it as the other goon began reaching for something in his pants. Lucky for me, goon #2 was just a bit more of a useless asshole than myself, and he just couldn't get his weapon out in time. As he struggled to take aim at me, I, a broken down wounded old man on his knees in a puddle of another man's face, managed to toss the ring and nail him right between the eyes. Upon impact, his entire head exploded like a popper full of confetti on New Year's Eve. Amen. Fuck me. Holy shit!

There was no music in the air following this showdown, like you'd expect—only the hum of doom seemed to hover in the night—and when the distant cry of sirens began to approach, I knew it was high time to start living up to my word, which meant that I would have to give the Red Beast to Betterton for all the trouble I had caused him.

. . . With the ring placed securely on my finger, I limped to my bad-assed and much missed Camaro, put it into gear with care, then crawled through the eerie barren streets of Las Vegas as I thought about all the places I'd like to go, just as soon as I drove back to Los Angeles.

## ABOUT THE AUTHOR

*Miguel Lasala is originally from southwestern Louisiana. He holds a Master of Architecture degree from the University of Louisiana at Lafayette, and has worked professionally in the field of architecture in New York City, Los Angeles, Texas, and Louisiana. This is his first book.*